Finding Wild

By Megan Wagner Lloyd
Pictures by Abigail Halpin

Alfred A. Knopf New York

For Seth — M.W.L.

For Mom and Dad — A.H.

THIS IS A BORZOI BOOK PUBLISHED BY ALFRED A. KNOPF

Visit us on the Web! randomhousekids.com

Educators and librarians, for a variety of teaching tools, visit us at RHTeachersLibrarians.com

Library of Congress Cataloging-in-Publication Data
Lloyd, Megan Wagner.
Finding wild / Megan Wagner Lloyd ; illustrated by Abigail Halpin. — First edition.
pages cm.
"This is a Borzoi book."
Summary: "All the ways and places that wild exists in our world and where you can find it."
—Provided by publisher
ISBN 978-1-101-93281-0 (trade) — ISBN 978-1-101-93282-7 (lib. bdg.) — ISBN 978-1-101-93283-4 (ebook)
[1. Nature—Fiction. 2. Senses and sensation—Fiction.] I. Halpin, Abigail, illustrator. II. Title.
PZ7.1.L59Fi 2016
[E]—dc23
2015003024

The illustrations were created using watercolor, and colored pencil, and finished digitally.

MANUFACTURED IN MALAYSIA
July 2016
10 9 8 7 6 5 4 3 2 1

First Edition

Random House Children's Books supports the First Amendment and celebrates the right to read.

What is wild?
And where can you find it?

Wild is tiny and fragile and sweet-baby new.
It pushes through cracks and crannies
and steals back forgotten places.

Sometimes wild is so tricky,
you have to squint to see it.

And then there are times you
can't possibly miss it.

Wild *creeps*
and *crawls*
and *slithers*.
It leaps and pounces
and shows its teeth.

Wild is full of smells—fresh mint, ancient cave,
sun-baked desert, sharp pine, salt sea.
Every scent begging you to drink it in.

Wild is forest-fire hot
and icicle cold.

It's as smooth as the petals of poppies, and as rough as the fierce face of a mountain.

WATCH OUT!
Wild can hurt.
Itch!
Burn!

OUCH!
Sting!

But wild can also soothe:
gentle breeze, cheering sun, soft rain.

Wild keeps many secrets, waiting to be discovered—
like its candy: honey from bees and sap from trees,
swift-melting snowflakes and juice-bursting blackberries.

Wild roars and barks and hisses and brays.

It storm-thunders and wind-whispers.

Wild sings.

Sometimes wild is buried too deep, and it seems like the whole world is clean and paved, ordered and tidy.

You look and look, and all you can see are streets and cars and buildings so high, they hide the sky.

1
N → 2.5
NE → .5

And then,

just when you are about to give up—

There.

There it is again.

Old and worn and
still standing strong—

Wild.